Celebrate

By Christine Reynebeau

Illustrated by Kimberly Wix

Published by Dreambuilt Books
Printed in the USA.

Wausau, WI 54403

Show Your Love and
Leave a Note:

To all my people who celebrate my wins and give me roots in the storms; may each of you know that your love matters and is worth celebrating!

Wedding days are filled with love,

flowers, dancing,
and sometimes a dove.

Marriage is an important promise

And they've selected
YOU

to stand alongside them

when they say,

" I do"!

She'll be in a dress,
a stunning bride she will be!

He'll be mighty handsome in his suit,
just waiting to see.

Every guest will come all dolled up,
and ready to choose a side,

invited to celebrate this big day
with the Groom and Bride.

The wedding party is filled with people who are important to the pair,

asked to stand at the alter, as people who have always been there.

The ring bearer brings the rings
to the front of the room.

He makes sure they're ready for the bride and groom.

The flower girl
walks ahead
of the beautiful
bride,

presenting her with flower petals
spread from side to side.

They'll promise to
stand together on
the bad days,

and celebrate the
good ones too.

This day is just the beginning

of a life they'll build together.

You're a special person in the first day of their forever!

So celebrate and dance with joy,
until the songs come to an end,

because love is important in marriage, family, and friends!

It's the roots that keep you grounded when life sends you a storm,

And the feeling that
keeps your
heart open and warm!

So when you find someone that you love to the moon...

it's very important
to celebrate that happiness
with everyone in the room!

The End

Other Titles:

PB & J

GUTS

KIND

RESCUE

visit dreambuiltbooks.com